Plated Armor

By Darren W. Freeman

Table of Contents

Chapter 1

Thinking back to the one night that changed everything about being a cop... It was 2020, and I had been wearing the badge for just over a year. Being a police officer was a calling I had always felt deep down, but in truth, it wasn't just about duty—it was about proving myself. Proving that I belonged, that I could hold my ground, and that I was someone people could count on when it mattered most. I didn't know it then, but that night would test everything I thought I knew about loyalty, courage, and justice.

I arrived at the station that evening with the same routine as every shift. The smell of coffee and paper greeted me as I stepped inside. Officers filed into the briefing room, chatting about mundane things—family, football scores, plans for their next day off. I remember how normal it all felt, how disconnected those conversations were from what would happen later.

The briefing room itself was its usual chaotic self. Someone had left a stack of newspapers on one of the desks, and the bulletin board in the corner was cluttered with missing person flyers, crime stats, and faded motivational posters. The room buzzed with energy, but as I took my seat, I felt a strange sense of unease. It wasn't a sharp alarm—more like a dull thrum in the back of my mind, as if something in the air had shifted.

Sgt. Watson strode in a few minutes later, carrying his tablet in one hand and a paper cup with coffee in the other. He didn't need to command attention; his sheer presence was enough. Watson was a veteran through and through—broad-shouldered, gravel-voiced, and always straight to the point.

"Alright, listen up," he barked, silencing the low chatter. "Tonight's shifts are routine for most of you. But I've got something special for Stiles and Mike." He jabbed a finger in our direction, his eyes locking onto mine for a beat longer than usual.

I straightened in my chair, suddenly feeling the weight of his gaze. Stiles, sitting beside me, gave a slight nod, unfazed as always. He was the steady one between us, the seasoned partner who never seemed rattled, no matter the situation.

Watson continued, "We've had an uptick in activity at the waterfront. Illegal smuggling—people, drugs, cash. The usual suspects. Homeland Security issued an alert earlier today. They're worried about cartel involvement."

The room seemed to chill at the mention of the cartel. We'd all heard the stories. Cartels didn't just deal in drugs; they dealt in power, ruthlessness, and silence. If they were working the waterfront, it wasn't small-time stuff.

"Your job," Watson said, "is to patrol the pier and keep your eyes open. If you see something, you call it in. No heroics. You hear me?"

"Yes, sir," I said automatically, though a flicker of doubt tugged at the edge of my thoughts. The pier was always an eerie place at night—too many shadows, too many blind spots. And the idea of cartel involvement added a layer of danger that made my stomach twist.

Watson's gaze softened, just for a moment. "You two are solid. I wouldn't send you down there if I didn't think you could handle it. But be smart. That's all I'm asking."

Stiles leaned over as Watson moved on to the next topic. "You look nervous," he said, his voice low and calm.

"I'm fine," I lied. "Just not a fan of the pier."

Stiles grinned. "Well, you've got me watching your back. And don't forget—prayer works. I said mine before I walked in here."

I rolled my eyes, but I couldn't help smiling. Stiles had a way of making everything seem manageable. He wasn't just my partner; he was my anchor.

By the time the briefing ended, the sky outside had darkened completely, and the city had settled into its usual nighttime rhythm. The streets were quiet as Stiles and I walked to our patrol car, the faint hum of streetlights blending with the distant sound of waves lapping against the pier.

"You ever get a bad feeling about a shift?" I asked as we slid into the car.

"All the time," Stiles replied, fastening his seatbelt. "But I've learned one thing over the years: gut feelings are worth listening to, but they don't tell the whole story. The job's not about feeling—it's about focus."

I nodded, trying to absorb his calm confidence. "Guess I'll try to focus, then."

As we pulled out of the lot, the city unfolded before us—rows of darkened storefronts, the occasional bar with its neon lights flickering, a handful of cars passing by on their way home. Everything looked so ordinary, so normal. But the unease lingered, like a faint shadow I couldn't shake.

The clock on the dashboard read 10:47 p.m. as we drove through the dimly lit streets, the city winding down for the night. Most people were in their beds, blissfully unaware of the unseen world that came alive after dark. For us, though, this was when the job truly began.

Our first few calls were routine—nothing to raise the blood pressure. A noise complaint from a cranky neighbor turned out to be a late-night movie blasting through thin apartment walls. A suspicious person loitering near a closed gas station was just a teenager waiting for his ride. Each call ended with the same humdrum resolution: nothing to worry about, nothing to report.

"Starting to think this bad feeling of yours is just rookie jitters," Stiles teased as we drove away from the gas station. He leaned back in his seat, his hands resting lightly on his lap. The radio crackled softly, filling the silence between us.

"Maybe," I admitted, though I wasn't convinced. "But you ever notice how quiet the city feels some nights? Like... too quiet?"

Stiles chuckled, shaking his head. "You watch too many movies, kid. Quiet's a blessing in this line of work. Trust me, when things get loud, that's when you've got problems."

I didn't answer. I wanted to believe him, but I couldn't shake the sense that the quiet tonight wasn't peaceful—it was waiting; watching.

The pier loomed ahead as we turned down the narrow road that led to the waterfront. Rows of warehouses lined the stretch of crumbling asphalt, their darkened windows like empty eyes staring out at the ocean. Beyond them, the water gleamed faintly under the moonlight, its surface shifting with the tide.

"Looks like we're here," Stiles said, his tone lighter than the moment deserved. He clicked off the car's headlights as we rolled to a stop near the pier entrance. The engine hummed softly, a steady pulse in the oppressive silence.

We had a system for patrolling the pier. It wasn't official protocol, just something we'd developed over time. One of us would go on foot, moving between the warehouses, while the other stayed in the car, circling the area. It made it harder for anyone to spot us coming, and it usually worked. Usually.

"I'll take foot patrol," Stiles said, popping the door open. "You play chauffeur."

"Fine by me," I replied, though I didn't envy his part of the job. The pier at night was no place for comfort. Every creak of the wood, every shadow cast by the moon, felt like something alive, ready to pounce.

Before stepping out, Stiles grabbed his flashlight and turned to me. "Stay sharp, Mike. And switch to the tac channel. We don't want anyone listening in."

I nodded, adjusting my radio as Stiles disappeared into the darkness.

I eased the car forward, rolling slowly down the length of the pier. With the headlights off, the darkness was nearly absolute, broken only by the faint glow of the moon and the scattered streetlamps that barely lit the area. The water lapped gently against the wooden posts beneath the pier, the sound unnervingly loud in the stillness.

I scanned the area carefully, my eyes darting from shadow to shadow. Every movement—a flicker of light, the sway of a rope—set my nerves on edge.

I kept the windows down, letting the salty air fill the car. It wasn't comforting, but it was grounding, a reminder that this was real.

The radio crackled to life. "Mike, turn around," came Stiles' voice, calm but clipped. "I've got something."

I stiffened, my pulse quickening. "What is it?" I asked, my hand already moving to shift the car into reverse.

"Group of guys," he said. "Five of them, behind the far warehouse near the fence. Four with backpacks. They saw me coming and tried to hide."

"Copy that. On my way."

I swung the car around, driving back the way I came before pulling over near the warehouse Stiles had mentioned. The unease I'd been feeling all night hit me full force as I stepped out of the car. The air seemed thicker here, heavy with something I couldn't name.

Climbing over the six-foot fence, I landed with a soft thud on the other side. The faint sound of footsteps guided me toward the back of the warehouse, where I found Stiles standing with his gun drawn. His flashlight beam illuminated a group of five men kneeling on the ground, their hands raised in surrender.

"WTF, Stiles?" I muttered, my voice low but urgent. "What's going on?"

Stiles didn't look at me. His focus remained locked on the men. "Caught them trying to duck behind the building. Four of them have backpacks. Check this out."

Keeping his weapon trained on the group, Stiles motioned to one of the bags. I crouched down, unzipped it, and froze. Staring back at me were bricks of cash, neatly stacked and tightly wrapped.

"Jesus," I whispered. "How much is this?"

"No idea," Stiles said, his tone grim. "But it's enough to make this feel very wrong."

The men didn't say a word, but their expressions spoke volumes—fear, desperation, and something else I couldn't quite place. One of them, the only one without a backpack, seemed different. His eyes weren't darting around like the others'. He was watching. Calculating.

Before I could say anything, the distant hum of engines broke the stillness. I looked up sharply as two unmarked SUVs appeared at the edge of the pier, their red and blue lights flashing faintly from behind the grilles.

"Crap," I muttered. "Unmarked cars. Stiles, who the hell are these guys?"

Stiles didn't reply. His stance stiffened, and his eyes tracked the SUVs as they rolled to a stop about fifty feet away, their headlights casting harsh, angular beams against the pier's dark surroundings. The low rumble of their engines faded into an unnatural stillness as the vehicles idled, their exhaust curling in the chilly night air.

The doors clicked open, and five men stepped out with military-like precision. They moved with practiced ease, their tactical vests snug against their bodies, weapons strapped to their sides. One of them, a tall, broad-shouldered man with a trimmed beard, took the lead. Even in the faint light, his air of authority was palpable.

"Stay back!" Stiles barked, his flashlight beam sweeping across the group. The men squinted as the light cut through the shadows, but none flinched. They spread out slightly, their movements coordinated but not overtly aggressive.

One of the men raised his hands slightly, a gesture meant to diffuse tension. "Relax, officers," he said, his voice steady and composed. "We're on your side."

My stomach twisted at his words; it didn't feel like they were on our side. I glanced at Stiles, whose grip on his weapon didn't waver.

"Our side, huh?" Stiles replied, skepticism lacing his tone. "How about you flash some ID?"

The lead man nodded toward one of his companions, who unzipped a pouch on his vest and pulled out a slim badge wallet. The leader mirrored the action, holding up an identical badge. "Homeland Security," he said firmly. "We've been tracking this group for weeks. This is our operation."

Chapter 2

Stiles didn't drop his weapon. He stood firm, his gaze locked on the men, his grip tightening on the flashlight, his finger still hovering near the trigger. The badge-wielding agent's words hung in the air, but something about the way they moved and spoke felt wrong. There was a chill in my gut that wouldn't go away.

Homeland Security?

I glanced again at the five men. The lead agent, the one calling the shots, had a face that could belong to anyone in this field—sharp jawline, eyes like steel, a faint smile that didn't quite reach his eyes. He wasn't the kind of guy who showed up in a situation like this without a damn good reason. But something about their lack of coordination with local law enforcement didn't sit well with me. And neither did their unmarked vehicles.

"Homeland Security, huh?" Stiles said again, his voice flat, not buying it. He didn't lower his gun. He didn't even flinch. "Funny how you don't bother to let us know you're running an op."

The lead agent, Special Agent Carter, let out a dry chuckle. "We work fast, Officer. Sometimes faster than local agencies can keep up."

Stiles didn't respond. His eyes were still locked on Carter, scanning every inch of the group behind him. The other agents seemed calm, too calm—too controlled. But it was the men we had detained that made my skin crawl.

One of them, the one without the backpack, was watching the agents intently, his eyes flicking from one to another with a careful, almost calculated precision. I couldn't help but notice the way his hands were shifting, the subtle gestures he was making—almost like he was signaling.

A shiver ran down my spine.

"Stiles, you see that?" I murmured, keeping my voice low but tense. My eyes remained trained on the man without the backpack.

Stiles followed my gaze and frowned. "Yeah. I don't like it."

I took a small step forward, keeping my weapon in hand, but my mind raced. What the hell was going on? Why was this guy acting like he had a plan? Why was he signaling to them, like they were all in on something?

I glanced back toward Agent Carter, who was still holding his ground, his eyes sharp. He didn't seem to notice, or maybe he was just pretending not to. Either way, he wasn't going to let us stall for long.

I pulled my hand from my holster, keeping my fingers close to the grip, but not drawing my gun just yet. "I'm calling this in," I said, trying to sound more confident than I felt. "We're not going anywhere until we talk to my watch commander."

Without taking my eyes off the men, I fumbled for the radio on my belt. My heart began to race as I keyed it up and waited for the familiar crackle of static. But it didn't come. I keyed it again. And again. Silence.

"What the hell?" I muttered under my breath, frustration gnawing at me. I keyed the radio one more time, pressing the button harder, hoping for a response, but still, nothing. Not even a pop of static.

Stiles, noticing my growing concern, turned his head slowly toward me. "Let me guess. Radio's jammed?"

I nodded, my pulse quickening. "Yeah. Something's not right here. this isn't some routine bust. They're blocking our comms."

Agent Carter's expression didn't change, but I saw the faintest glimmer of something—something smug—flash in his eyes. The other agents were watching, too, their eyes moving from Stiles and me to the men on the ground, then back to each other.

"Like I said, Officer," Carter spoke up again, his voice smooth, almost too smooth. "We've got this under control. We've been tracking these smugglers for weeks. We don't need your help." He took a step closer, his tone turning more clipped, more authoritative. "We don't need any more questions. We need you to step aside. Now."

There it was. The underlying threat. I could feel it hanging in the air, thickening by the second.

I tightened my grip on the radio, not bothering to hide my frustration. "I'm not stepping aside. We'll wait for my supervisor. He'll handle this."

At my words, the atmosphere shifted. Carter's cool demeanor remained, but the men around him tensed imperceptibly. Their hands hovered near their weapons, ready. Too ready.

"We'll deal with it when my supervisor gets here," I said firmly. "I'm not moving until I get confirmation. You can't just pull us out of the loop like this. It's not how this works."

There was a long beat of silence. My stomach was in knots, my instincts screaming that this wasn't just a miscommunication. This was something more. Something dangerous. I didn't trust these men, and I didn't trust the situation.

And then it happened—so fast I barely saw it coming.

The agent to Carter's right—young, with a sharp buzz cut—suddenly jerked his hand toward his weapon. His gun came out in one fluid motion, the barrel glinting in the dim light.

I barely had time to react.

The deafening crack of gunfire rang out, and Stiles—Stiles—collapsed to the ground with a sickening thud, the force of the bullets slamming into his chest.

"No!" I shouted, dropping to a crouch beside him. I could see it all in slow motion—the flash of the muzzle, the dark streak of blood blossoming on Stiles' chest as he was knocked backward.

Stiles went down hard, the impact of the bullets sending him sprawling across the gravel, his body armor taking the brunt of it. But still—three rounds. Even with the vest, it couldn't have felt good.

I didn't even think. I just reacted.

I fired.

It was instinct. My hand moved almost before my brain could process what was happening, the gun in my hand barking as I fired off two shots. The first bullet caught the agent in the shoulder, and he stumbled back, cursing under his breath. The second shot missed, but the force of the exchange sent the group into disarray.

The agents immediately ducked behind their cars, taking cover as the sound of gunfire echoed in the silence of the waterfront. My heart pounded in my chest as I took cover behind a nearby crate. My eyes darted back to Stiles, who was groaning, clutching his chest where the bullets had struck.

I didn't have time to check if he was okay. The agents were moving, crouching low, their eyes scanning the surroundings as they tried to regain the upper hand. I could feel the heat of their weapons even from here, their presence closing in like a storm.

I didn't wait for the next shot.

"Stiles!" I shouted, dragging him by the arm. He groaned again, struggling to get his feet under him, but the adrenaline kicked in. I pulled him toward the nearest warehouse, the one closest to the pier, and shoved him through the door.

Inside, it was dark and musty, the smell of old wood and rust lingering in the air. I didn't have time to be cautious. We had to move, and we had to move fast.

I dragged Stiles further inside, kicking the door shut behind us as I slammed it with my foot. The loud thud of the door hitting the frame echoed through the warehouse. The others—those detained—were already inside, huddled in the shadows, their eyes wide with fear.

I reached for my radio again, but with the comms still blocked, I cursed under my breath.

It was just us now. The calm before the storm had turned into a battle for survival. The agents' voices could be heard muttering outside, but they hadn't made any moves to enter yet. I knew it wouldn't be long before they regrouped and came at us again. They had the firepower. They had the numbers. And now they had us cornered.

I slammed my back against the wall, eyes scanning for any sign of an escape route. We couldn't stay here long.

Stiles groaned again, still holding his chest, but his eyes locked onto mine. "What now?" he whispered hoarsely, his voice barely audible above the pounding in my ears.

I didn't answer right away. I couldn't. The weight of the situation pressed down on me like a vice.

But there was one thing I knew for sure: we were in deep, and we weren't getting out without a fight.

Chapter 3

The heavy warehouse door slammed shut behind us, the metallic clang reverberating like a death knell. My lungs burned as I leaned back against it, trying to steady my breathing. Outside, the faint crunch of gravel under boots echoed, each step a chilling reminder that the nightmare wasn't over. I tightened my grip on my sidearm, the weight in my hand feeling both reassuring and terrifying.

"Stiles, you okay?" I asked, glancing over at him. He was slumped against a stack of wooden crates, his breaths shallow but even. His hand pressed tightly over his chest, right where the rounds had struck.

"Yeah," he muttered through gritted teeth. "The Good Old Plated Body armor held up. Feels like I got kicked by a damn mule, though."

A surge of relief mixed with anger coursed through me. Relief that he was alive—anger at the people outside who had tried to take him from me. I pushed it down, knowing it wouldn't help now. The sound of his voice was enough to steady me, even if only for a moment.

The warehouse was dark and smelled of rust and salt. Moonlight filtered through a few shattered windows high above, creating jagged streaks of light that did little to chase away the shadows. The silence inside was unnerving, broken only by the ragged breathing of the men we'd brought in with us.

They huddled together near a stack of pallets, their faces pale, their eyes darting around like caged animals. Four of them clung to each other, whispering frantically in Spanish, but one sat apart from the group—the man who hadn't been carrying a backpack. Raul, I'd learned his name was. His posture was tense but calm, his sharp eyes darting toward the door and then to me.

"What the hell are we supposed to do now?" I muttered under my breath, not expecting an answer. My mind raced, a dozen scenarios playing out, none of them good. Stiles shifted, wincing, and the sound snapped me back to the moment. "We can't stay here forever."

"Mike," Stiles rasped, cutting through my thoughts. "They're going to come for us. They're not just going to walk away."

I swallowed hard, trying to suppress the panic rising in my chest. He was right. Every instinct I had told me that the men outside weren't just going to let us walk away. They'd made their play, shown their hand. And now, it was survival of the fittest.

My eyes scanned the warehouse, taking in the rows of rusted machinery, broken crates, and tangled wires. It was a relic of better days, long since abandoned, but it was the only thing between us and the armed men who wanted us dead. The walls were thin, the windows fragile. This wasn't a stronghold—it was a coffin.

"Mike," Stiles said again, pulling me out of my spiraling thoughts. His voice was softer now, calmer. "We've been in bad spots before. We've gotten out of them. We'll get out of this."

I nodded, though his words felt hollow. This wasn't like anything we'd faced before. This wasn't a simple drug bust or a routine disturbance call. This was a conspiracy, layered in corruption and soaked in blood money, and we were caught in the middle of it, unarmed backup, outnumbered, and outgunned. I'd seen fear before—on the streets, in the eyes of criminals and victims alike. But this time, it was my own fear staring back at me.

I turned my attention to Raul. He hadn't said much since we got inside, but there was a look in his eyes—a mixture of fear and something else. Determination, maybe. Or desperation. He wasn't just an innocent bystander caught in the wrong place at the wrong time. He knew more than he was letting on.

"You," I said, stepping closer. "Start talking. What's going on here?

He hesitated, his dark eyes flicking to the door and then back to me. For a moment, I thought he wasn't going to answer. Then he sighed, running a hand through his hair.

"My name is Raul," he said. "I used to work for them. For the cartel."

The air in the room seemed to shift, the tension thickening like a storm cloud. Stiles straightened slightly, his eyes narrowing. I felt my grip tighten on my gun, every muscle in my body screaming at me to stay on edge.

"You worked for the cartel?" I repeated, my voice colder now. "And we're just supposed to believe you're not part of this mess?"

"I didn't have a choice!" Raul snapped, his voice rising. "They forced me. Threatened my family. I was just an accountant—a numbers guy. I didn't want any of this."

"And yet, here you are," I said, my tone sharp. "Caught in the middle of a smuggling operation with corrupt agents and millions of dollars in cash."

Raul flinched, but he didn't back down. "I was trying to escape. That's why they're after me. I saw too much—too many things they didn't want anyone to see."

The fear in his voice was real, but it didn't make me trust him. Not yet. I exchanged a look with Stiles, whose skeptical expression mirrored my own.

"And those hand signals?" I shot back, my voice laced with suspicion. "You were signaling to them— don't think I didn't notice. What were you doing?"

Raul froze, his eyes widening slightly. "No, no," he said quickly, shaking his head. "That wasn't what you think. I wasn't signaling them—I was warning them."

"Warning them?" I scoffed. "About what?"

"About you!" Raul said, his voice sharp now. "About the fact that you weren't in on it. They thought you were part of the setup, just more corrupt cops who would play along. When you didn't, they panicked. That's why they jammed your radios. That's why they tried to kill you."

I exchanged a skeptical look with Stiles. His face was pale, but his eyes were sharp. Raul's story fit, but it didn't mean he was innocent.

My stomach turned at his words. If he was telling the truth, it meant this whole operation was bigger than I'd imagined. The men outside weren't just after Raul—they were cleaning up loose ends. And we'd walked right into their trap.

Raul hesitated, then leaned closer, lowering his voice. "They're moving cash—millions of dollars— through this port. And they're using people like them—" he gestured to the group behind him—"as cover. Migrants, families, anyone desperate enough to take the risk. They pack them into the shipments, mix them with the money, and send them through."

"And those agents outside?" I asked, dreading the answer.

"They're not agents," Raul said. "Not really. They're on the payroll. The cartel buys them to protect shipments, silence anyone who gets in the way."

The weight of his words hit me like a gut punch. "You're saying Homeland Security agents are on the cartel's payroll?"

Raul nodded. "Not all of them. Just enough to keep things running smoothly. The cartel doesn't take chances. They've bought politicians, law enforcement, even the military in some places. This is just business to them."

I looked at the frightened faces of the detainees, most of them too scared to speak or even move. They weren't just unlucky bystanders caught in a raid. They were pawns in a game I hadn't even realized I was playing.

Corrupt agents, cartel operatives, and now we were caught in the crossfire.

Raul's words rattled in my mind like loose bullets in a tin can. They'll box us in first. Seal off any escape routes. Then they'll hit us hard. The warehouse around us suddenly felt smaller, the air thicker.

I looked at my phone again, wanting the signal bars to reappear, but the screen remained stubbornly blank. No service. No lifeline. No hope of backup.

Stiles groaned. "And we thought tonight was just gonna be a routine bust."

Raul's eyes darted to the window, his expression grim. "They won't rush in. They'll surround the building, cut off every exit, and come at you from all sides." It felt like he could hear my thoughts.

I scanned the warehouse again. It wasn't defensible—just a thin-walled coffin waiting to be nailed shut. I spotted a service door in the back, half-hidden by crates. "That door," I said, pointing. "It might lead to an alley. If we can slip out—"

"They've got the perimeter covered," Stiles interrupted. "You know they do."

"Then we need a distraction," I said. "Draw them to one side while we slip out the other."

Raul shook his head. "Too risky. They're better armed, better prepared."

"Better than sitting here waiting to die," I shot back.

Before Raul could respond, static crackled faintly, followed by muffled voices. I froze, my ears straining. It was faint but unmistakable—radios.

Raul moved back to the window, peering cautiously through the gap. "They're talking on radios," he said. "I can't make out what they're saying, but they're moving. Organizing."

I joined him at the window, keeping low as I scanned the dark lot outside. The headlights of the unmarked cars cast long shadows across the ground, and the silhouettes of men moved purposefully in the gloom.

"They're setting up for an assault," I said, my stomach tightening.

Stiles groaned, shifting uncomfortably on his crate. "How long do you think we've got?"

"Not long," Raul said, his voice grim. "They'll want to hit us hard and fast before we have time to come up with a plan."

I stepped away from the window, my mind racing. We were outnumbered, outgunned, and completely cut off. But giving up wasn't an option.

"We'll have to improvise," I said, my voice steadier than I felt.

Chapter 4

We moved quickly, though every step felt weighed by the oppressive quiet of the warehouse. The old machinery and broken crates that had once seemed like obstacles were now potential lifelines— makeshift cover, obstacles to slow them down, traps if we were lucky enough to set them right.

Stiles worked beside me, his movements stiff and deliberate. He winced with every twist of his torso, the body armor having absorbed the brunt of the shots earlier, but it hadn't left him unscathed. I watched him out of the corner of my eye, noting the beads of sweat on his brow and the slight tremor in his hands. He was pushing through the pain, same as always. But he wasn't at his best.

"Let's stack those crates near the main entrance," I said, my voice low. "They won't stop a bullet, but they'll make anyone coming in think twice."

Stiles nodded without a word, hefting a smaller crate and dragging it toward the door. His silence was unsettling. Normally, he'd crack a joke to lighten the mood, even in the worst situations. Now, there was nothing but the heavy scrape of wood on concrete and the occasional grunt of effort.

After a few minutes, he finally spoke. "Mike...
what if we're wrong?"

I paused, wiping sweat from my brow with the
back of my hand. "About what?"

"About all of this." He gestured vaguely at the
warehouse, at the crates, at the looming threat
outside. "They're wearing badges. They've got
government-issued gear. What if we're about to
start a firefight again with federal agents?"

"They're not agents," I said firmly. "Not really.
You heard Raul. They're cartel muscle, bought and
paid for. Badges don't mean anything when they're
working for the highest bidder."

Stiles let out a shaky breath, sinking onto one of
the crates. He rubbed a hand over his chest, where
the rounds had hit him earlier. "Yeah, but what if it's
not that simple? What if some of them don't know
what they're part of? What if they're just following
orders, same as we do?"

I crouched down in front of him, meeting his
gaze. "And what happens if we don't fight back?
What happens if we let them walk in here and take
Raul and the others? They'll kill them, Stiles. They'll
kill all of us. We don't have the luxury of second-

guessing ourselves right now." They Fucking shot first!!

He looked away, his jaw tightening. "I never thought I'd have to shoot at people wearing the same uniform as us."

"I know," I said softly. "But those uniforms don't mean what they should anymore. You've seen it yourself—the corruption, the cover-ups. We're not fighting the badge. We're fighting the people who've twisted it into something ugly." I will kill everyone of them.

Stiles nodded slowly, though his shoulders remained tense. "It just... doesn't sit right."

"Nothing about this situation sits right," I admitted. "But we didn't start this. We're just trying to survive it."

We worked in silence for a while longer, fortifying the entrance and blocking off the more obvious points of entry. I found a length of old chain and used it to secure one of the side doors, looping it through the rusted handles and tying it off with a piece of metal piping.

As we moved through the warehouse, I kept glancing toward the detainees. They were huddled together, whispering among themselves. Raul stood apart, his gaze flicking between us and the darkened windows.

"Raul," I called out, motioning him over. "Anything you can tell us about their tactics? How they'll move?"

He approached cautiously, his hands tucked into his pockets. "They'll surround the building first. Cut off every exit. Then they'll hit hard and fast, hoping to overwhelm you before you have a chance to react." I have seen them kill others before.

"Great," Stiles muttered. "So we're sitting ducks."

"Not necessarily," Raul said, glancing around the warehouse. "If you make it difficult for them—slow them down, make them question what's inside— they'll be more cautious. They won't want to risk their own lives."

I nodded, considering his words. "Then we need more than just barricades. We need to make it look like we've got more firepower than we do."

Stiles perked up at that, a glimmer of his old self shining through. "Decoys?"

Raul nodded. "Or use sound. Echoes. Make them think there's movement all over the place."

As we worked, Stiles seemed to relax a little, throwing himself into the task. He even cracked a smile when one of the crates toppled over, sending a cascade of metal parts clattering to the floor.

"Think they'll fall for it?" he asked, wiping his hands on his pants.

"They don't need to fall for it completely," I said. "They just need to hesitate long enough for us to find a way out."

Raul leaned against a nearby crate, watching us with a wary expression. "You really think you can outmaneuver them?"

"I think we have to," I said. "We're not getting out of this by waiting for a miracle."

Stiles nodded, his expression hardening. "Then let's make sure they regret ever walking through that door."

We finished our makeshift defenses, stepping back to survey our work. It wasn't much, but it was better than nothing.

I wiped my hands on my pants, glancing at Stiles. He looked exhausted but determined, his usual grin replaced by a grim set to his mouth. We were in this together, no matter what.

"We need more distractions," I said. "Smoke. If we can create a smokescreen, it'll buy us time."

Stiles rubbed his chin thoughtfully. "You thinking about those old fire extinguishers we saw in the corner?"

"Exactly." I crossed the room and grabbed two of the extinguishers. They were old, the labels faded, but they still felt full. "We pop these off when they make their move. Fill the room with smoke and confusion."

Raul watched us, a flicker of admiration in his eyes. "It might just work."

"It's gotta work," I said. "Because I'm out of other ideas."

As we sat down to catch our breath, the weight of the situation settled over me again. We were outnumbered and outgunned. But we weren't out of options.

Not yet.

I glanced at my watch, noting the time. We couldn't afford to wait much longer. The men outside were already organizing, planning their next move. We had to stay one step ahead. I was just so shocked that no one had heard the shots that were fired.

"I'm going to check the perimeter again," I said, rising to my feet. "Make sure they haven't shifted positions."

Stiles nodded, rubbing his hands together. "Be careful."

I moved through the shadows, careful to stay low and out of sight. At the back of the warehouse, I peered through a crack in the wall, my heart pounding as I spotted movement in the distance. Figures moved like shadows, circling the building. They were patient, methodical. They weren't going to rush in blindly.

Good. The longer they took, the more time we had to prepare.

Returning to the main floor, I found Stiles tinkering with an old workbench, rigging up a crude tripwire using some loose wiring and a rusted wrench.

"Nice," I said, nodding in approval. "That might give us a heads-up."

"Or scare the hell out of us," Stiles said with a wry smile. "Either way, it's better than nothing."

Raul joined us, his expression somber. "They'll come in soon. Once they think you're vulnerable."

"Then we make sure we're ready," I said, my voice firm. "This isn't about winning. It's about surviving."

Stiles clapped me on the shoulder, his grip steady despite the tremor I knew he was fighting. "Let's give them hell."

"Damn right," I said, tightening my grip on my weapon. We weren't just sitting ducks. We were cornered wolves—and we were ready to fight.

Raul cleared his throat. "There's something you need to see," he said, pulling a worn satchel from under his coat. He unzipped it slowly, glancing nervously toward the windows as though expecting someone to burst in at any moment.

He pulled out a thick folder, the papers inside yellowed and crinkled at the edges. He spread them out on a nearby crate, tapping a finger on one of the documents. "This is why they want me dead."

I leaned in, my eyes scanning the first page. It was a list of names, dozens of them, along with photos and brief descriptions. Many of the names had government titles beside them—customs agents, police officers, even a few judges.

"These are the people working with the cartel?" I asked.

Raul nodded. "They've been on the payroll for years. Some of them don't even realize it—they think they're just cutting corners, accepting harmless bribes. But others... they know exactly what they're doing. They're the ones who make sure shipments get through ports unnoticed, who silence witnesses, who erase evidence."

Stiles picked up another page, his expression darkening as he read. "This is... this is huge. There's no way this doesn't go straight to the top."

"It does," Raul said grimly. "The man in charge— he's a high-ranking official. He uses his position to protect the cartel's interests. That's why they're so desperate to find me. If this information gets out, it'll blow their whole operation wide open."

I flipped through the pages, taking in the sheer scale of the corruption. There were shipping manifests, bank statements, even emails detailing backroom deals. Everything was meticulously documented.

"They were sloppy," Raul said, noticing my incredulous expression. "They got comfortable. They never thought anyone would dig this deep."

"And now they're scrambling to cover their tracks," I said.

"Exactly." Raul tapped a photo paperclipped to one of the documents. It showed a man in a suit, shaking hands with someone I recognized—a known cartel leader. "This is the proof we need. If we can get this to the right people, we can bring the whole thing down."

Stiles leaned in, studying the photo. "And who exactly are the 'right people'? We can't trust anyone inside. Not with something this big."

Raul hesitated, then pulled out a flash drive from his pocket. "That's why I made backups. Multiple copies. Hidden in different places. We just need to survive long enough to get to one of my contacts."

I met Stiles' gaze, a silent understanding passing between us. The stakes had just gotten a whole lot higher.

Stiles frowned, glancing at Raul. "How'd you even get your hands on this stuff? Something this big—it's not like they'd just leave it lying around."

Raul leaned against a stack of crates, his face shadowed by the dim light. "They didn't. I had access because I used to manage logistics for one of their shell companies. They trusted me because I didn't ask questions—until I started connecting the dots."

Stiles folded his arms. "And they didn't notice you taking copies of their files?"

"They're not careless," Raul admitted. "But they're arrogant. They never thought anyone on the inside would turn against them. They were so busy covering their tracks with law enforcement, they forgot to watch their own people."

I rubbed my temples, feeling the tension mounting. "You're telling me you built this dossier under their noses?"

Raul nodded. "Piece by piece. At first, I was just keeping it to protect myself. But then I realized it was bigger than that. The only way to stop them is to expose them."

Stiles muttered under his breath. "Damn."

Raul pulled a flash drive from his pocket and handed it to Mike. "This is a copy. One of many. It's encrypted and geo-locked to my phone. If something happens to me, it'll wipe itself clean."

I took the drive and slipped it into my pocket. "Then we'll make sure nothing happens to you." I tapped the folder, a sense of urgency creeping into my voice. "We need to get this to someone we can trust. Someone outside their reach."

Raul nodded. "I know a journalist. Independent. She's been chasing this story for years. If anyone can blow the lid off this, it's her."

"Then we've got a mission," I said. "First, we survive. Then, we make sure the truth gets out."

Before anyone could say anything in response, a low thud echoed from outside the warehouse.

I froze, holding up my hand. "You hear that?"

Stiles nodded, his hand instinctively reaching for his weapon. The thud came again, followed by the faint crunch of gravel.

"They're here," Raul whispered.

I grabbed the fire extinguishers we had rigged as smoke screens. "Stiles, get ready. We stick to the plan. Tripwires, smokescreen, fallback positions."

Stiles nodded, shaking off the lingering doubt. "Let's give them a reason to regret this."

The warehouse fell into a tense silence, broken only by the sound of approaching footsteps and the crackle of radio chatter from outside.

Then, the first window shattered. The assault had begun.

Chapter 5

The sharp crack of gunfire echoed through the warehouse, shattering the tense silence. I instinctively ducked behind a crate, my heart pounding in my chest. Stiles scrambled beside me, wincing as he hit the floor hard. His armor might have saved his life, but it hadn't left him unscathed.

"What are we gonna do?!" one of the men we'd taken into custody shouted, panic in his voice. His name was Tuco, I think. He clutched his backpack like it was a lifeline, eyes darting toward the door.

"Stay down and keep quiet," I snapped, my voice harsher than intended. "You want to survive this, don't you?"

Tuco nodded quickly, his knuckles white as he gripped his bag. The other two detainees were huddled together, eyes wide with fear. They'd seen trouble before, but now they looked like scared kids caught in something way over their heads.

Stiles checked his weapon, his hands shaking slightly. "They're coming in hard. We need to slow them down."

I nodded, peering through a crack between the crates. Shadows moved outside, agents and cartel members working together to surround the warehouse. They were not like the usual gangbangers we dealt with. These guys knew what they were doing.

"We stick to the plan," I said, trying to keep my voice steady. "Let the traps do some of the work."

The first trap triggered with a loud bang—a tripwire Stiles had set earlier. The explosion wasn't lethal, but it sent a spray of metal shards and debris into the air. Shouts of surprise and pain followed, and I allowed myself a grim smile.

"Got 'em," the mother fuckers", Raul muttered, a hint of satisfaction in his voice. "That'll make them think twice."

"Don't get cocky," I warned. "They'll regroup fast."

Sure enough, more gunfire peppered the warehouse, bullets punching through the thin metal walls. One round ricocheted off a nearby pipe, sending a shower of sparks raining down. The smell of gunpowder filled the air, acrid and suffocating.

Raul crouched beside us, his face pale but determined. "They're trying to flush us out. They'll use any force they have to."

"Let them try," I said, gripping my Glock .40 Caliber tighter. "We're not going down without a fight."

The sound of glass shattering drew my attention to the back of the warehouse. Another one of the windows had been broken from the outside, a canister landing with a dull thud. Smoke began to pour from it, thick and choking. They still had not tried to fully enter.

"They've got gas!" Stiles yelled. "We need to deploy our own smokescreen now."

I nodded, grabbing the old fire extinguishers we'd prepped earlier. "Time to see if these still work."

Stiles grabbed one as well. We moved to the edges of the main floor, away from the direct line of fire. With a quick twist of the nozzle, I released a thick plume of white smoke into the air. The extinguisher sputtered at first, but then roared to life.

"Keep it going!" I shouted. The smoke spread quickly, mingling with the gas pouring in from the attackers. Soon, the entire warehouse floor was engulfed in a dense, blinding haze.

I could hear confused shouts from outside, men coughing and stumbling in the smoke. The attackers' careful coordination broke down as they struggled to navigate through the chaos.

"They're disoriented," Stiles said, coughing as he moved beside me. "They can't see us either."

"Good. That's exactly what we need."

One of the attackers tried to rush through the side door, but he tripped over a wire we'd set, crashing to the floor with a loud grunt. Another stepped into one of the tripwires that released a cascade of debris from above. The combination of confusion and physical obstacles was working better than we'd hoped.

"We need to keep them off balance," I said, adjusting my grip on the extinguisher. "Let's move to the back and regroup."

We herded the detainees toward the rear of the warehouse, guiding them through the smoke-filled maze. The air was thick, and every breath burned my lungs, but we kept moving. The agents continued to fire blindly into the building. We returned fire

driving back any potential assault back into the
building.

At one point, Raul stumbled, nearly dropping his
satchel. I grabbed his arm, pulling him back to his
feet. "We need that evidence," I reminded him.
"Don't let it go."

"I won't," he gasped, clutching the bag tighter.

As we pushed further into the warehouse, I could
hear the attackers regrouping outside. They were
still out there, but the smokescreen had bought us
precious time.

"Seal that door!" I ordered, pointing to a metal
loading dock door. Stiles and Raul helped me shove a
heavy shelf in front of it, creating a makeshift
barricade.

Tuco and the other detainees huddled nearby,
their faces pale and terrified. "We're trapped, man.
We're trapped like rats."

"Shut up," I snapped. "Keep it together."

Another explosion rocked the warehouse, this
one closer. The floor shook beneath my feet, and I
felt the heat of the blast wash over me. Flames

licked at the edges of the smoke, turning the warehouse into a fiery maze.

"They're trying to burn us out," Raul said grimly.

"We can't let them," I said. "There's too much evidence here. If it all goes up in flames, we've got nothing."

Stiles glanced toward the spreading fire, sweat streaming down his face. "We need to push further back. There's another storage area past the loading dock. We can regroup there."

"Go!" I ordered, waving the detainees forward. "Stay low and move fast."

We navigated through the chaos, the smoke thickening with every step. The heat was unbearable, and I could feel my clothes sticking to my skin, soaked with sweat. Every breath burned, my lungs screaming for clean air.

At the rear of the warehouse, we found a small storage area filled with old equipment and supplies. It wasn't much, but it provided some cover. We collapsed behind a stack of crates, gasping for air.

Tuco and the others were coughing violently, their eyes wide with fear. "We're gonna die here," one of them muttered, his voice shaky.

"No, we're not," I said firmly. "We're gonna survive this. We just need to hold out a little longer."

Raul looked around, "Anyone hit?"

"We're good," Stiles said, wiping sweat from his brow. "But that fire's spreading fast."

Before we could catch our breath, another round of gunfire erupted outside. The attackers weren't giving up.

"We need a new plan," I said, my mind racing. "We can't just sit here and wait for them to break through."

Stiles nodded. "We have to think like them. They expect us to be scared, desperate. Let's use that to our advantage."

Raul frowned. "How?"

"Diversion," Stiles said. "Make them think we're trying to escape through another exit. Draw them away from the main entrance."

I glanced around the storage area, my eyes landing on an old forklift. "That could work. We rig the forklift to crash through the side wall, make it look like we're making a run for it."

Stiles grinned despite the situation. "You always did like smashing things."

"Desperate times," I said with a shrug. "Let's do it."

We worked quickly, rigging the forklift to move on its own. Raul found a piece of metal piping to wedge the accelerator down, while Stiles and I cleared a path through the crates.

"Ready?" I asked, glancing at the others.

Tuco and the detainees nodded nervously. "What about us?" Tuco asked. "What do we do?"

"Stay here and keep your heads down," I said. "We'll handle the rest."

With a final push, we sent the forklift rumbling toward the side wall. It crashed through with a deafening roar, debris flying everywhere. The sound echoed through the warehouse, masking our own movements.

"Now!" I yelled. "Move further back!"

We retreated deeper into the storage area, using the confusion to our advantage. The smoke and fire were spreading fast, but we were still alive.

For now.

Chapter 6

The sound of coughing was the first thing I noticed as the adrenaline from the firefight began to ebb. It was a harsh, rattling noise, like dry leaves being crushed underfoot, and it came from one of the detainees. I turned to find Tuco hunched over, clutching his chest as his body convulsed with each labored breath.

"Tuco, you okay?" I asked, my voice rough from the smoke that had clawed its way into my throat.

He shook his head, his face pale beneath the grime and soot. "Can't... breathe," he managed between coughs. His words came out in wheezes, barely audible over the crackling fire in the distance.

Stiles knelt beside him, his own face tight with concern. "He's taken in too much smoke. We need to get him some fresh air."

I scanned the room, taking stock of our surroundings. The storage area we'd holed up in was a maze of old equipment and forgotten supplies, the air thick with heat and the faint smell of mildew. Outside, the fire and smoke had likely driven back our attackers for the time being, but it wouldn't last. We had a moment to regroup, no more.

"Fresh air's not an option right now," I said grimly. "But we've got a bit of time to figure something out. Let's see what we're working with here."

Stiles nodded, though his eyes lingered on Tuco for a moment longer. The other detainees were huddled nearby, their faces drawn with fear and exhaustion. One of them, a wiry guy named Carlo, was trying to fan Tuco with his hands, though it wasn't doing much good.

"Stay calm," I said to the group. "We'll get through this."

I didn't know if I believed my own words, but I had to keep them focused. Fear was as dangerous as the fire and smoke. I motioned for Stiles to join me, and we started combing through the room.

The storage area was a graveyard of old equipment: rusted tools, broken crates, and dusty shelves stacked with unidentifiable junk. I grabbed a flashlight from my belt, its beam cutting through the gloom, and began searching for anything useful.

"What are we even looking for?" Stiles asked, his voice low as he opened a nearby cabinet. Inside were a handful of cracked glass jars and a coil of rope that disintegrated when he touched it.

"Anything that gives us an edge," I replied. "Supplies, a way to communicate—hell, even something to block the smoke."

We moved methodically, the urgency of the situation keeping us silent. Stiles found an old toolbox, its contents mostly rusted beyond use, but he pocketed a screwdriver and a pair of pliers anyway. I unearthed a stack of tarps that could be useful for sealing off the worst of the smoke if it came to that.

Then I saw it.

On a high shelf, half-hidden behind a stack of cardboard boxes, was a radio. Not the sleek, modern kind, but one of those old-timey models with dials and an antenna that looked like it belonged in a World War II bunker. My heart skipped a beat.

"Stiles," I called, pointing toward the shelf. "Help me get this down."

He turned, his eyes following my gesture. "You think it still works?"

"There's only one way to find out."

Together, we maneuvered the heavy device down to the ground. The radio was caked in dust, its once-shiny surface dulled by years of neglect. I brushed it off with my sleeve, revealing the faded lettering on the dials. It looked old enough that it might operate on frequencies the cartel's jammers couldn't block.

"Think you can get through to the precinct?" Stiles asked, crouching beside me as I started fiddling with the knobs.

"Maybe," I said. "If this thing still has any life in it."

The power switch gave a satisfying click as I flipped it on. For a moment, nothing happened, and my stomach sank. Then, a faint hum filled the air, followed by the crackle of static.

"It's working," I said, relief washing over me. "Let's see if we can find an open frequency."

I adjusted the dials, my fingers moving with a mixture of hope and desperation. The static shifted, rising and falling in a rhythm that made it feel like the radio was breathing. I cycled through channels, searching for anything that sounded like a human voice.

"Central to 5-4, do you copy?" I said into the microphone, my voice steady despite the chaos around us. "This is Officer Mike Harris, requesting immediate assistance. Over."

Nothing but static.

"Try another channel," Stiles urged. He glanced toward the detainees, who were watching us with a mix of hope and apprehension. Tuco was slumped against the wall, his breathing still shallow but steady for now.

I switched frequencies and tried again. "This is Officer Harris, requesting backup at the warehouse on 22nd and Main. Hostile forces on-site. Do you copy? Over."

The static wavered, teasing the possibility of a response, but no voice came through. I tried channel after channel, my frustration mounting with each failed attempt. Finally, I slammed my hand against the side of the radio, the dull thud echoing in the small room.

"Damn it!" I muttered, running a hand through my sweat-drenched hair. "They've jammed everything. Even this old thing can't break through."

Stiles placed a hand on my shoulder, his expression grim but steady. "At least we tried. It's more than we had before."

"Doesn't feel like much," I said, my voice bitter. I looked around the room, the weight of our situation pressing down on me. The fire outside was still burning, and our attackers were likely regrouping. Time was running out, and we were no closer to finding a way out.

"What now?" Stiles asked.

I exhaled heavily, forcing myself to focus. "We need to keep moving. If they come in here and we're boxed in, we're done for."

"What about Tuco?" Stiles glanced at the detainee, who was now leaning against Carlo for support.

I hesitated. Tuco was in bad shape, but leaving him behind wasn't an option. "We'll figure something out. Let's search the rest of this place. Maybe there's something we missed."

Stiles nodded, and we split up again, combing through the remaining shelves and cabinets. I found a stack of old blankets, which might help with the smoke, and a few bottles of water that were probably expired but still sealed. Stiles came back with a fire extinguisher and a roll of duct tape, both of which could prove invaluable.

As we regrouped, I caught sight of Raul examining the radio. "You think you can get it to work?" I asked, hope flickering faintly.

Raul shook his head. "The hardware's fine, but if they're jamming the signals, there's not much we can do."

I nodded, though it felt like another nail in our coffin. "Then we focus on getting out. The fire might keep them at bay for a little while, but it's also cutting off our exits. We need to find another way out of here."

The detainees looked at me, their eyes filled with unspoken questions. They weren't cops, and they hadn't signed up for this. But they were in it now, and their survival depended on us.

"We stick together," I said, meeting each of their gazes. "We'll find a way out. But I need you to trust us and do exactly as we say."

Carlo nodded, his grip tightening on Tuco's arm. "We're with you."

For now, that was enough. The air was heavy with tension, but I pushed it aside. We weren't out of this yet, but we were still alive. And as long as we were breathing, we had a chance.

The radio had been our last hope for outside help, and with it dead in the water, our options were dwindling fast. The fire outside crackled ominously, its heat bleeding into the walls, and the faint sounds of movement from the attackers suggested they were regrouping.

"We can't just sit here," I said, more to myself than anyone else. "We need a way out."

Raul, who had been leaning against the far wall, suddenly straightened. "There might be another way."

"What do you mean?" Stiles asked, wiping soot from his face.

Raul motioned toward the back corner of the room, where an old tarp lay crumpled on the ground. "I saw something earlier when we were searching. There's a hatch under that tarp. Might be worth a look."

I exchanged a glance with Stiles. "Why didn't you mention this before?"

Raul shrugged, looking sheepish. "Didn't think much of it. But if there's a chance it leads somewhere..."

Without wasting another second, I crossed the room and yanked the tarp away, revealing a heavy steel hatch embedded in the floor. The metal was scratched and dented, its edges worn smooth with age. A rusted padlock hung from the latch, but it looked brittle, as if it might snap under the right pressure.

"Looks like some kind of smuggling tunnel," I said, crouching to examine the lock. "Could be our ticket out of here."

Stiles knelt beside me, running a hand over the hatch. "If it's still intact, it might lead out of the warehouse. But we need to make sure it doesn't lead straight into a cartel hideout."

"Point taken," I said. "Let's get it open first."

Using the tools we'd scavenged earlier, I managed to pry the padlock apart with a satisfying crack. Stiles and I heaved the hatch open, the hinges groaning in protest. A wave of cool, musty air wafted up, a stark contrast to the heat and smoke above.

The tunnel below was dark and narrow, the faint outline of wooden supports barely visible in the flashlight's beam. It stretched downward at a slight angle, disappearing into the shadows.

"This is it," I said, my voice tinged with cautious hope. "This could be our way out."

I crouched near the hatch, running my fingers along its edge. "If this tunnel's no good, we're out of options."

Stiles leaned against the wall, his eyes darting between the hatch and the door. "Even if it's usable, we've got a problem. We leave this open, they'll follow us in. We shut it tight, and we're cutting off our only escape route."

Raul cleared his throat. "The tunnel's been here for years. It might still lead somewhere, but there's no guarantee it's clear or stable. Someone needs to go down first and check."

"Fine," I said, nodding. "I'll go."

Stiles frowned, shaking his head. "Not happening. You're the one holding this group together. If something happens to you down there, we're done. I'll check it out."

"You're injured. If something…" I began to argue, but his expression stopped me. Stiles wasn't one to throw himself into danger lightly. If he was volunteering, it wasn't up for debate.

"Take a flashlight," I said, handing mine over. "And be quick about it. We don't know how much time we've got."

Stiles accepted the light with a curt nod. He knelt by the hatch and swung his legs into the opening, disappearing into the shadows. The sound of his boots hitting the tunnel floor echoed faintly. For a moment, the room fell silent, save for the crackle of distant fire and the occasional cough from one of the detainees.

Raul shifted nervously. "You really think this will work?"

"I don't know," I admitted. "But we don't have much of a choice."

Carlo, still propping up Tuco, spoke up. "What about them?" He jerked his chin toward the door. "Even if we get out, they'll just come after us."

"That's why we need a plan to slow them down," I said, glancing around the room. "We need to buy ourselves enough time to get clear."

Raul rubbed the back of his neck, his expression skeptical. "What can we do? We're outgunned and outnumbered."

"Doesn't mean we're helpless," I replied. "We've already rigged one trap. We can set more."

Stiles' voice drifted up from the hatch, startling us. "Tunnel looks clear so far. It's tight, but it's holding. I'll go a bit further and see if it opens up."

"Be careful," I called back, my chest tightening with worry. Stiles wasn't just my partner; he was my anchor. If something happened to him down there...

I shook the thought from my head and turned back to the group. "We don't have much, but we've got enough to make their lives miserable if they try to storm in here."

I gestured toward the scattered debris around us: broken crates, old fire extinguishers, and a few half-empty paint cans. "We can rig more distractions, create choke points. Anything to slow them down."

Carlo frowned. "You really think that'll stop them?"

"No," I admitted. "But it doesn't have to. It just has to buy us time."

Raul knelt beside a pile of metal scraps, picking up a jagged piece of rebar. "I can set up something at the door—make it look like the room's booby-trapped. Might make them hesitate."

"Good," I said. "Anything that keeps them guessing."

Stiles' voice came again, this time louder. "Tunnel opens up after about fifty feet. Looks like it heads downhill, maybe toward the river."

I exhaled a breath I didn't realize I'd been holding. "That's something, at least."

"It's tight, though," Stiles added. "We'll have to go single file. If they follow us, it won't take much for them to box us in."

I glanced down the hatch, the shadows seeming to stretch endlessly. His words hung in the air, heavy and undeniable. It was a gamble to use the tunnel, but staying here wasn't an option either.

"Come on, let's get you back up here," I said, extending my hand toward Stiles.

He hesitated for a fraction of a second, his gaze flickering between the tunnel and me, before grabbing my hand. His grip was firm, but his palm was clammy. I hauled him up with a grunt, and he landed on the floor beside me, brushing dirt from his knees.

"The tunnel's our best shot," he said, looking around at the rest of the group. "But we've got to make sure they don't follow us. If they figure out where we went, it won't take long for them to catch up."

The detainees shifted nervously, their eyes darting toward the door where the faint sounds of movement could still be heard. I caught a glimpse of Tuco slumped against Carlos's shoulder, his face pale and slick with sweat. Time wasn't on our side.

"Let's focus," I said, trying to project calm even though my pulse was racing. "We need to make it look like this room is more trouble than it's worth."

"Traps worked before," Carlo offered, his voice unsure. "We could rig something again."

I shook my head. "They'll be expecting traps this time. If we try the same thing, they'll see through it."

Stiles rubbed his chin thoughtfully. "Then we need something bigger. Something that screams, 'Don't come in here.'"

The room fell silent as we all racked our brains for ideas. My gaze swept across the mess of old equipment and debris scattered around us. There had to be something we could use—anything to make this place look like a death trap.

"Maybe we fake it," I said finally. "Make them think this whole place is rigged to blow."

Stiles raised an eyebrow. "And how exactly do we do that?"

I opened my mouth to respond, but before I could, Stiles' eyes narrowed, his attention snagged on something in the corner. He walked over, crouching beside a stack of rusted metal drums. When he stood up, he was holding a bundle of thick, frayed cables, their ends capped with what looked like ancient connectors.

"What've you got there?" I asked, stepping closer.

Stiles held up the cables, a slow smile spreading across his face. "Fake explosives."

I frowned, not following. "What?"

"These cables." He shook them for emphasis. "They look just like detonation cords. If we spread them around, tie them to a few of these drums, and throw in some blinking lights, it'll look like we've rigged the place to blow sky-high."

I stared at the cables, the idea starting to take shape in my mind. "It's not a bad plan," I admitted. "But we'll need more than just cables to sell it."

"There's plenty of junk in here," Stiles said, already scanning the room. "We can use the fire extinguishers for pressure tanks. Maybe some of those old tools for 'detonators.' We just need to make it look convincing."

Raul stepped forward, his brow furrowed. "You really think they'll fall for it?"

"They don't need to believe it for long," I said. "Just long enough for us to get out of here."

The group set to work, the urgency of the situation overriding any lingering doubts. Stiles took the lead, directing us like a man possessed. He had a knack for improvisation, and it showed as he pieced together the fake bomb setup with alarming speed.

We arranged the cables in an intricate pattern, snaking them around the room and tying them to the rusted drums. Stiles found an old toolbox filled with small, blinking LEDs—probably from some outdated machinery—and rigged them to the cables. When the lights blinked, they looked startlingly authentic, like the countdown timers you'd see in a Hollywood thriller.

"Nice touch," I said, watching as he taped one of the LEDs to a drum.

"Yeah, well, let's hope they don't look too closely," he replied, his tone grim. "This'll only work if they don't have time to figure out it's fake."

Meanwhile, the detainees and Raul worked on spreading debris near the door to make it look like the room was already primed for detonation. They stacked crates haphazardly, creating the illusion of a hasty setup. Tuco, still too weak to do much, watched from his spot against the wall, his breathing shallow but steady.

"Almost done," Stiles said, stepping back to survey his work. "We just need one more thing to sell it."

"What's that?" I asked.

"A trigger," he said, pointing to the center of the room. "Something obvious. A big red button or a switch. They need to believe we can blow this place with the push of a button."

I frowned, glancing around. "We don't have anything like that."

"We improvise," he said, his eyes scanning the clutter. His gaze landed on an old industrial breaker switch mounted on the wall. "That'll do."

We pulled the switch from the wall and wired it to one of the blinking LEDs. When it was done, it looked like something straight out of a spy movie—a crude but convincing control panel for a makeshift bomb.

"Looks good," Raul said, stepping back to admire the setup. "Scary, even."

"Good," Stiles said, wiping sweat from his brow. "Scary's what we're going for."

The room was silent for a moment as we all took in the scene. The blinking lights, the snaking cables, the ominous switch—it was a work of art, in a grim sort of way.

"Now what?" Carlo asked.

I glanced at the door, the muffled sounds of movement on the other side reminding me that our time was running out. "Now we make our move. We head down the tunnel and seal the hatch behind us. If they come in here, they'll think twice before touching anything."

"And if they don't buy it?" Raul asked.

"They will," Stiles said, his voice firm. "But we'll be long gone before they have a chance to test it."

I nodded. "Let's pack up and get moving. The sooner we're out of here, the better."

The group moved with renewed urgency, gathering what little they could carry and preparing to descend into the tunnel. The fake bomb might not hold them off forever, but it was the best chance we had.

As we lowered ourselves into the hatch, one by one, I couldn't shake the feeling that we were leaving behind more than just a room full of junk. We were leaving behind the last vestiges of control in a situation that had spiraled far beyond anything I'd ever imagined.

Chapter 7

The moment I lowered the hatch behind me, the air shifted, thick and stale with the scent of damp earth and old rot. It was a stark contrast to the heat and smoke we had just escaped. Everyone looked shaken, sweat mixing with the grime and soot clinging to their faces, but we were alive. That had to count for something.

Then, above us, we heard it—the unmistakable sound of footsteps.

They had entered the storage room.

Everyone froze. No one dared to move. Even our breathing seemed too loud in the suffocating quiet of the tunnel.

Muffled voices filtered through the wood and debris above, sharp and urgent.

"They were just here!" someone barked, frustration edging his words.

"Search everything," another ordered. "They couldn't have gone far."

My grip tightened around the flashlight. The air in the tunnel was heavy, damp, but the heat of adrenaline still burned beneath my skin. We had expected this moment. The trap we'd left behind— our last gamble—was the only thing keeping them from storming after us. But it had to hold.

We couldn't afford for them to figure out the truth.

I cast a glance at Stiles, crouched beside me, jaw set, his breathing shallow. The others were packed in behind us—Raul, Carlo, Tuco, and the rest of the detainees. Some of them were still wheezing from the smoke, their ragged breaths almost painful to hear in the tight quarters of the tunnel.

Then, the voices above grew louder.

"The hell is all this?"

A pause. Then another voice, nervous, uncertain.

"Looks like… detonators?"

My pulse pounded against my ribs.

It was working.

A nervous chuckle followed. "Shit, do you think they actually rigged this place?"

Then, a deeper voice, one laced with skepticism. "It's probably a bluff."

The wood above creaked as someone shifted their weight.

"But what if it ain't?" another chimed in. "If they set charges and we go poking around, we could bring the whole damn place down."

A long silence stretched between them, as if they were all staring at each other, none of them wanting to be the idiot who tested the theory.

I let out the faintest, controlled exhale.

A part of me had worried they'd call our bluff immediately, but fear was a powerful thing, and no one wanted to be the first to make a mistake that could cost them their life.

Then, a sharp, commanding voice cut through the chatter.

"Leave it!" the leader snapped. "If it's a trap, we don't need to be screwing around with it. Fan out—

check the perimeter. If they're not here, they've already slipped out."

Footsteps shuffled above, a mix of hesitation and retreat. I could imagine them now—fanning out into the warehouse, weapons drawn, scanning every shadow for movement. Some of them would be frustrated, others relieved that they wouldn't have to find out whether the supposed explosives were real or not.

Then came the moment of truth.

A long pause.

The hatch creaked ever so slightly as someone stepped near it.

My entire body went rigid.

If they opened it, if they so much as tried—

But they didn't.

The leader made a sound of irritation. "Forget it. We'll find them another way. Let's go."

The footsteps receded.

We stood there, silent, waiting. The only sound was the distant echo of their boots scuffing against concrete, growing fainter with each passing second. Then… nothing.

I forced myself to count. Ten seconds. Twenty. Thirty. A full minute.

No one dared speak until I finally turned to the group and whispered, "They're gone."

A few of the detainees let out shaky breaths of relief. Tuco, still hunched over and pale, sagged against Carlo, who gave his shoulder a reassuring squeeze.

"They bought it," Carlo muttered, more to himself than anyone else.

"Yeah, for now," Stiles said, voice hushed. He didn't look relieved, though—just tense, eyes still locked on the ceiling above us. "But they're not stupid. They'll figure it out if they don't find us anywhere else."

I nodded. "Then we need to move. Fast."

I turned, shining my flashlight deeper into the tunnel. The walls were damp stone, the ceiling arched just enough that I had to hunch slightly as I moved forward. The ground was uneven, slick in some places with condensation. It smelled of old earth, rust, and something faintly metallic.

Raul cleared his throat. "You really think this tunnel leads somewhere?"

I didn't answer right away. The truth was, I had no damn clue.

"It has to," I said, because we didn't have another option.

The tunnel stretched ahead into darkness, its end swallowed by shadow. The beam of my flashlight barely cut through the thick air, revealing only damp stone walls slick with condensation and the rusted rail tracks beneath our feet. The air was different down here—heavy, still, carrying the scent of earth, mildew, and something metallic, like old blood.

I swallowed against the unease creeping up my spine. We had no idea where this tunnel led, no clue if it opened up somewhere safe or if we were just walking ourselves into a dead end.

But we didn't have a choice.

"We move," I said, more to myself than anyone else. "Stay close."

No one argued. There wasn't anything left to say.

The space was tight—too tight for comfort. We had to walk single file, our shoulders nearly brushing the curved stone walls. The ceiling was low, forcing some of us to hunch slightly as we moved. Every sound was amplified—the scrape of boots against dirt, the faint dripping of water somewhere unseen, the shallow, labored breaths coming from behind me.

Tuco.

I turned my head just enough to glance back. He was leaning against Carlo, his face barely visible in the dim light. He looked worse than before—his breathing ragged, chest rising and falling too quickly like he couldn't get enough air.

"Tuco," I said quietly. "You hanging in there?"

"Yeah," he rasped, but even that one word sounded like it took effort.

Carlo tightened his grip around Tuco's side, keeping him steady despite the narrow space. "He needs air," he muttered. "We gotta find a way out of here soon."

I nodded, even though we both knew we couldn't make that happen any faster.

Tuco wasn't the only one struggling. The detainees were exhausted, their bodies running on whatever scraps of adrenaline were left after everything we'd been through. Stiles, leading up ahead, was moving carefully but quickly, his flashlight scanning the ground for anything that might trip us up. Raul and another detainee, a woman named Mia, followed closely behind, their faces set with quiet determination.

The deeper we went, the more the darkness felt alive, pressing in around us like a weight. The tunnel twisted slightly, curving just enough that we could never see too far ahead.

"How long do you think this thing goes?" Raul murmured, voice low as if speaking too loudly would wake something in the walls.

"No idea," I admitted. "Could be a hundred feet. Could be a mile."

Silence followed, thick with the unspoken thought: And what if it's blocked?

No one wanted to say it, but it hung in the air between us, a constant threat. If the tunnel collapsed somewhere up ahead—if we hit a dead end—there was no turning back. We'd be trapped.

Tuco coughed again, this time worse than before. His body shook with the effort, and Carlo had to stop walking for a second just to keep him from falling over.

"Damn it," Carlo hissed under his breath. "We need to slow down."

"We can't," Stiles said from up ahead, voice firm but not unkind. "Not here. We need more space before we can stop."

Carlo let out a frustrated breath but kept moving, one arm wrapped tight around Joel to keep him from collapsing.

We walked in silence after that, only the sounds of our breathing and footsteps filling the void. The tunnel walls seemed to close in, the weight of the unknown pressing against us from all sides.

And still, we kept moving.

We had been walking for at least twenty minutes, maybe more. Down here, in the depths of the tunnel, time felt like it had lost all meaning. There was nothing but the rhythmic crunch of our boots on dirt, the occasional cough from Tuco, and the steady hum of our own breath, thick with exhaustion.

Then the path ahead narrowed suddenly.

Stiles stopped short, lifting his flashlight higher. The beam trembled slightly as it fell upon a collapsed section of the tunnel. The ceiling had caved in at some point, leaving behind jagged slabs of stone and twisted metal beams that jutted out like broken ribs.

"Shit," Raul muttered. "Can we even get through?"

Stiles stepped forward, testing the stability of the debris. "Looks like we can, but it's gonna be tight." He turned back, his expression grim. "We'll have to squeeze through one at a time. No way around it."

I exhaled sharply and looked at the others. Most of them were already exhausted, barely holding on. Tuco was in no shape to be crawling through rubble, but we didn't have a choice.

"Alright," I said. "Let's make it quick."

One by one, we maneuvered through the collapsed section, pushing past jagged edges and loose rock. The space was tight, too tight. I felt my shoulders scrape against stone, my arms pinned close to my sides as I wormed my way through. The weight of the fallen debris above me made my breath hitch—it felt like the whole thing could come crashing down at any second.

Somewhere behind me, I heard Tuco groan as Carlo tried to help him through. "Easy, man," Carlo said, his voice strained. "Almost there."

Stiles, who had gone first, crouched on the other side, reaching back to help pull people through. His flashlight flickered suddenly, the beam sputtering in and out.

"That's not good," I muttered.

He smacked the side of it a couple of times, and the light steadied, but the concern was clear in his expression. "If this dies, we're screwed."

"Anyone else got a light?" I asked, glancing at the others.

Raul pulled out a small keychain flashlight, but it was weak, barely more than a dim glow. "Better than nothing," he said with a shrug.

The thought of walking in complete darkness sent a cold shiver down my spine. There was no telling how long this tunnel stretched, and if our lights failed before we reached the end, we'd be feeling our way through blind.

"Let's keep moving," I said, pushing away the thought. "One thing at a time."

By the time we all made it past the collapsed section, we were gasping for breath, our bodies coated in dust. The air was even staler now, thick and dry, making it harder to breathe.

My throat ached, my stomach knotted with hunger. And judging by the looks on everyone else's faces, I wasn't the only one.

"Anyone got anything left in their bags?" I asked.

Raul slung his backpack off his shoulders and dug through it. Another detainee the same. Between the two of them, they came up with a couple of cereal bars and a handful of trail mix.

"Not much," Carlo admitted. "But it'll keep us going."

I nodded. "Let's walk a little farther, find some space to sit for a few minutes. We can't stop here."

No one argued. We just kept walking.

Because there was no other way.

After what felt like an eternity of trudging through the suffocating tunnel, the space finally widened.

The walls, once pressing in on us like a closing fist, pulled back, opening into a slightly larger chamber. It wasn't much—just a break in the unrelenting passage—but it was enough. Enough for us to straighten our backs, roll the stiffness out of our shoulders, and breathe a little easier.

"Let's stop here," I said, already sinking down against the dirt wall. My legs were screaming for rest, my throat raw from thirst.

Stiles sat down next to me with a heavy sigh. Raul and Carlo helped Tuco ease himself down carefully, his face pale and drenched in sweat. The rest of the detainees slumped against the walls or the floor, their exhaustion palpable.

We passed around what little food we had. A couple of cereal bars. A handful of trail mix. Not enough to fill anyone's stomach, but enough to keep us moving. Enough to remind us we were still alive.

Tuco took a bite and chewed slowly, as if every movement cost him energy he didn't have. "Never thought I'd be eating trail mix in a smuggling tunnel," he muttered.

Stiles huffed a tired laugh, rubbing the dust from his face. "Yeah, well, I never thought I'd be crawling through one."

There was a brief silence. Then Stiles looked at the detainees, his expression shifting from exhaustion to something sharper. "Where exactly were these guys planning to take you?" he asked.

For a moment, no one answered. A few of them exchanged glances, uncertain. Then Mia spoke.

She had been quiet for most of the journey, keeping to herself. The only woman among the detainees, she was thin, her face smudged with dirt, her dark hair tied back into a loose, tangled braid. Her voice was hoarse when she spoke, but steady.

"They were moving us," she said. "We weren't supposed to stay in the city long. They told us we'd be safe, that they had work for us. That we'd have a better life."

I glanced at her. "And you believed them?"

Her lips pressed together, and for a second, I thought she'd lash out. But then her face softened, and she looked away. "When you have nothing," she murmured, "you believe anything that gives you hope."

Silence settled over us.

"I came here because my family needed me to," she continued. "My little brother is sick. My mother—she can't take care of him alone. I thought if I could find work, send money back..." Her voice broke, just slightly. "But it wasn't like that. When we got here, we weren't allowed to leave. They took our papers. Moved us from place to place. Told us if we tried to run, we'd regret it."

"Regret it how?" I asked.

Mia's jaw tightened. "They don't just kill you," she said. "They make you disappear."

No one spoke for a long moment.

I clenched my fists, feeling anger churn low in my stomach. I had seen this before—people taken in by false promises, trapped in something they couldn't escape. People used. Bought and sold. And no one ever talked about it until it was too late.

"They were splitting us up tonight," Mia said. "That's why we were at the warehouse. Some of us were being taken south, some of us west. They wouldn't tell us where."

"Human trafficking," Stiles muttered, shaking his head. "Jesus."

Mia exhaled shakily. "If you two hadn't come..." She let the thought trail off, but we all knew how it ended.

I ran a hand down my face. We had set out to bust a weapons deal. Now we were in the middle of something much bigger.

I looked at the others—tired, hungry, lost in an underground tunnel with no idea where it led. But at least we weren't in chains.

At least we were still free.

I swallowed hard, then pushed myself up. "We should get moving again," I said. "We don't know how long this tunnel is, and we can't afford to sit still for too long."

No one argued. One by one, we gathered our things and pressed forward, deeper into the unknown.

The tunnel didn't stretch on much longer.

After the endless crawl through the suffocating dark, the abrupt ending felt almost too soon, too sudden. We stopped, staring up at where the passage continued above us. The tunnel extended upwards into the unknown, disappearing into darkness.

"How the hell are we supposed to climb that?" Stiles muttered.

It was too high to simply give each other a boost, and the walls, though uneven, didn't seem to offer much of a handhold at first glance. The damp air around us felt heavier now, thick with the realization that if we couldn't find a way up, we might have just walked ourselves into a dead end.

I ran my hand along the rough stone wall, searching for anything—an edge, a grip, some foothold. My fingers brushed against something unexpected—small indentations, rough but deliberate.

"Wait," I said. I pressed my palm against the wall and moved my hand higher. More spaces. They were irregular but distinct, shallow holes in the rock, big enough to wedge a boot into.

"I think these are footholds," I said, glancing back at the others. "Probably made for climbing up."

Stiles stepped closer, running his own hand along the wall. "Yeah, looks like it. Think they were using this tunnel regularly?"

"Must've been," I said. "Smugglers, traffickers—they always have ways in and out."

I tested the first foothold, pressing my weight onto it. It held.

"Alright," I said. "I'll go first, make sure it's stable."

I started climbing. The uneven spaces were just enough to get a grip, though it took effort. My arms and legs burned with exhaustion, my muscles protesting with every push upwards. But the thought of being stuck down here kept me going.

After what felt like an eternity, I reached the top.

I pulled myself onto a flat surface and rolled onto my back, catching my breath. Once I had it, I sat up and lifted my flashlight, sweeping it across the space.

That's when I saw it.

At the end of the short passage ahead, a metallic door stood against the stone. It was old, worn, but sturdy. It looked like it hadn't been opened in a while.

I leaned over the edge. "It's safe! Come on up!"

One by one, the others climbed. Stiles followed first, moving quickly, then Carlo, helping Tuco as best he could. The detainees came last, their movements sluggish but determined.

Once everyone was up, Stiles and I moved toward the metal door.

"Keep quiet," I whispered.

I crouched down and ran my hand along the bottom edge of the door. There—a small gap. Barely big enough to peek through.

I lowered my head, pressing my cheek to the cold metal as I angled my flashlight off to the side to avoid giving away our position.

What I saw made my breath catch.

Beyond the door, we weren't in a city street or another warehouse. We were at the waterfront. The tunnel had led us away from the warehouse, just far enough that I could see the shimmer of water reflecting faint light from the docks. There were stacks of crates and shipping containers, the kind that could hide anything—or anyone.

Then I saw the movement.

Not a direct threat, not someone patrolling in the open. No, this was different. Shadows shifting. Someone staying low, trying to move without being seen.

Not one.

Several.

They were being quiet, just like us.

I pulled back, my heart pounding.

Stiles was already watching me. "What?" he asked, keeping his voice low.

I met his gaze. "We're not alone out there."

His jaw tightened. "You sure?"

I nodded. "They're moving carefully. Not running, not talking. Like they don't want to be noticed."

Stiles exhaled, looking back at the detainees. The reality of our situation settled over us like a thick fog.

We thought we'd made it out.

But we might have just walked straight into another trap.

Chapter 8

I exchanged a glance with Stiles, the weight of our situation pressing down on us. There was no way around it—no backup, no communication, no second chances. It was just the two of us against an unknown number of cartel reinforcements waiting on the other side of that metal door.

I inhaled slowly, steadying myself, and checked my gun. I had already used two magazines a few rounds outside the warehouse when they shot at Stiles. I wasn't sure exactly how many were left, but I'd counted enough shots to know I wasn't working with a full magazine anymore.

"How are you looking?" I asked Stiles, keeping my voice low.

He gave a nod and patted his vest. "Didn't fire all my rounds back there. Still got one full magazine."

That was something, at least. But even with his full magazine, it was two against... what? Five? Ten? More?

I hated fighting in the dark—both literally and figuratively.

I exhaled sharply, glancing back at the detainees. Their faces were lined with exhaustion, their clothes stained with sweat and dust from the tunnel. Tuco was barely holding himself up, leaning against Carlo, whose face was tight with concern. Mia's fingers twisted together, betraying the nerves she was trying to hide.

We couldn't take them with us. That much was obvious. They were weak, unarmed, and completely exposed. If we went out and got into a firefight, they'd be the first to go down.

I opened my mouth to say something when I noticed movement behind me. Raul. He had shifted slightly, his eyes darting to Stiles and then to me. His hand was gripping something inside his bag.

A bad feeling settled in my stomach.

"Raul," I said, my voice carefully measured. "What else is in the bag?"

His fingers tightened. He didn't answer right away.

"Raul." My voice came out harder this time.

Finally, he let out a slow breath and reached inside. My grip on my gun tightened on instinct, but

when his hand came out, I wasn't sure if I was
relieved or furious.

A gun.

Raul had a gun.

I didn't even have to look at Stiles to know he
was pissed. His whole body tensed beside me.

"You've had that this whole time?" Stiles hissed,
keeping his voice low but sharp.

Raul held up a hand like that would somehow
calm us down. "I— I needed it for protection."

I clenched my jaw, taking a step closer.
"Protection from who? Us?"

Raul looked between us, his face guarded. "I
didn't know if I could trust you," he admitted. "You
think I could just hand over my only defense when I
wasn't sure what your plan was? I didn't know if you
were actually going to help me or just use me for
what I knew and then leave me behind."

Stiles let out a harsh breath, shaking his head.
"We've been risking our necks for you. For all of you.
And you were hiding a damn gun?"

Raul lowered his gaze for a moment, shifting uncomfortably. "I wasn't sure about you guys at first," he muttered. "But I am now."

I wasn't sure if that was supposed to make me feel better. It didn't.

We didn't have time to argue about it, though.

I exhaled, forcing myself to focus on what mattered. "Fine. You have a gun. And now, we need a plan."

Stiles dragged a hand through his hair, turning his attention back to the metal door. "We can't take the detainees with us," he said, thinking out loud. "They'll just get caught in the crossfire. If we go out and they're behind us, they'll be sitting ducks."

I nodded. "We send them back down. Keep them safe."

I turned to face the group, who had been watching the exchange in tense silence. Their eyes flicked between me and Stiles, uncertain and anxious.

"You're going back downstairs," I said firmly, making sure my voice left no room for argument.

"Stay low, stay quiet, and don't come back up unless we come for you."

Mia swallowed, shifting on her feet. "What if you don't come back?"

The weight of the question pressed against my chest.

I met her gaze, keeping my voice steady. "We will."

She searched my face for a long moment before finally nodding.

One by one, they started moving back toward the tunnel opening. Carlo helped Tuco first, carefully guiding him back down as the others followed. Mia lingered for a second before disappearing into the darkness below.

Raul hesitated. He looked at me and Stiles, his expression unreadable.

"You better come back," he said quietly.

I nodded. "We will."

With that, he turned and followed the others down into the tunnel, vanishing into the shadows.

For a long second, it was just me and Stiles standing in the dimly lit space, staring at the metal door in front of us.

I tightened my grip on my gun.

"Alright," I murmured, more to myself than to him.

Stiles rolled his shoulders back and exhaled sharply, like he was shaking off the weight of everything behind us.

"No turning back now," he muttered.

I glanced at him. "Nope."

We both turned our eyes to the door.

Time to face whatever was waiting for us.

I pressed my back against the wall, gripping my gun tightly. The air was tense, the kind of tension that made your chest feel too tight, like the walls were pressing in. Stiles crouched low on the opposite side of the doorway, his fingers twitching slightly around his weapon. The distant sound of the water outside lapped softly against the docks, eerily calm in contrast to what was about to happen.

We were cornered. The cartel reinforcements were outside, and we had no idea how many. What we did know was that we were outgunned, outnumbered, and had no backup coming. The only way out was through.

Stiles exhaled through his nose. "They know we're in here. Question is, how patient are they?"

"Not very," I murmured.

We had one shot at this, and it had to count. We had no way out except through them.

Stiles glanced at me, reading my thoughts. "We don't have enough bullets to take them all out."

"I know," I said. "But they don't know that."

I reached into my pack and pulled out the length of rope we had scavenged earlier from the warehouse, tying one end securely around the handle of the metal door. I worked fast, looping it several times to make sure it wouldn't slip. Then, I took the other end and moved back, keeping myself flat against the wall.

"They'll fire the second the door moves," Stiles murmured, understanding the plan immediately.

"Exactly," I whispered.

I tightened my grip on the length of rope I had tied around the door handle. It wouldn't be enough to pull the door closed after we lured them into shooting, but that was fine. I had something else in mind for that.

I took a steadying breath and yanked the rope.

The door groaned, inching open just enough to reveal the darkness beyond.

The reaction was immediate.

Gunfire exploded through the open gap, deafening in the enclosed space. The cartel didn't hesitate, unloading round after round into what they assumed was our hiding spot. Bullets ricocheted off the walls, the metal sparking and clanging as stone and dust rained down around us.

Stiles and I stayed put, pressed flat against the walls, letting them waste their ammunition. I could hear them shouting to each other over the gunfire, some barking orders while others cursed under their breath.

Then, slowly, the shots dwindled.

Silence.

A pause thick with realization.

"They're not shooting back," one of them muttered outside.

"Bastards tricked us," another growled.

A few seconds later, I heard boots shifting on gravel, followed by a sharper voice. "Go check."

I glanced at Stiles. This was it.

We both gripped our weapons tighter as the cartel sent one of their men forward. His steps were careful, hesitant. He was smart enough to be wary, but he still had no idea what was waiting for him.

His shadow stretched through the narrow opening of the door as he stepped forward.

Closer.

Just a little more.

The moment I saw the barrel of his gun poke through, I moved.

I grabbed a thick metal rod I had found earlier—a rusted piece of piping left in the tunnel. I jammed it forward, slamming the door against his arm, pinning him in place for a split second. The man let out a sharp yell of pain, but he didn't have time to react before Stiles and I fired at the same time.

One shot to the chest. Another to the head.

He crumpled instantly, slumping halfway into the tunnel.

Shouting erupted outside.

"Shit! They got Marcos!"

"Get them! Now!" "End This"

More gunfire followed, but Stiles and I were already moving. I used the metal rod again, this time shoving the door back into place—not fully shut, but enough that we could control the gap. Just enough space to fire through.

And we did.

I took the first shot, hitting one of the cartel members in the throat as he tried to charge forward. He dropped instantly. Stiles was right behind me, his shot landing square in the chest of another man.

Chaos broke out among them. Some scrambled for cover, realizing they had no clear line of sight. Others fired blindly, hoping to hit something—anything.

A few bullets zipped past, close enough that I could feel the heat against my skin.

We kept going.

A third man fell to my shot, and I heard another curse as Stiles landed a hit on someone's leg, sending them sprawling. But there were still too many. And they had bigger guns.

The deafening sound of automatic fire roared through the night. Bullets hammered against the metal door, tearing through the stone around us. Shards of debris rained down, stinging my arms and face.

We ducked lower, trying to conserve what little cover we had left.

"They're pushing forward," Stiles shouted over the chaos.

I gritted my teeth, firing off another round. My gun kicked back in my hand, and I watched as another cartel member collapsed. But the moment of victory was short-lived.

Click.

My stomach dropped.

I was out.

I turned to Stiles just as I heard him curse.

Click.

The sound of his empty chamber echoed louder in my head than any of the gunfire before it. My breath caught in my throat as I met Stiles' eyes. He didn't need to say anything—I already knew.

We were out.

For a second, neither of us moved. The air between us was thick, heavy with exhaustion and the knowledge that we were standing on the edge of death. The cartel outside was still shifting, voices murmuring, their boots crunching against gravel. They were preparing for another assault. We had seconds, maybe less, before they came storming in.

And we had nothing left to fight back with.

I exhaled sharply, forcing myself to think. There had to be something—some last move, some last bit of strategy that could buy us another few seconds, another breath—

Then I heard it.

At first, it was just a distant hum, so faint that I thought my exhausted mind was imagining it. But then it grew. A vibration in the air, subtle but undeniable.

Engines.

Not one, but multiple.

The cartel outside must have heard it too, because their murmurs turned into sharp, hurried whispers. I caught a few words— shit, go, go, who the hell is that?

I pressed my ear against the thin gap in the door. Stiles did the same, his breathing shallow.

The next sound was even more unmistakable.

Tires skidding against gravel.

Doors slamming.

Then—

"State Troopers! Drop your weapons!"

The voice was sharp, commanding, cutting through the night like a blade.

I barely had a second to process it before everything outside erupted into chaos.

Gunfire exploded, rapid and precise. Not the reckless, panicked bursts we had been dealing with before. These were controlled shots, aimed and deliberate.

The cartel men outside lost their nerve almost instantly.

"What the hell—"

"We need to get out of here!"

"Where's the truck?"

"MOVE, MOVE—!"

Their panic was like wildfire, spreading through their ranks as they scrambled for cover. A few fired back, but it was clear they were outmatched.

The state troopers kept coming. I could hear the boots hitting the ground, the synchronized movement of officers working in formation. More voices rang out:

"Suspects running westbound—cut them off!"

"Keep them pinned—don't let them reach the boats!"

Another burst of gunfire, followed by a scream.

Stiles and I exchanged a look, still frozen in place. My pulse hammered in my throat.

Then, cautiously, I pushed the door open just enough to see.

The first thing that hit me were the flashing red and blue lights reflecting off the water, distorting in the ripples like a surreal painting.

Then the figures—officers in tactical gear, moving like a well-oiled machine as they advanced.

And the cartel?

Most of them were either dead, wounded, or scrambling into the night like roaches when the lights came on.

A few still tried to resist, firing off shots as they ran, but they were picked off one by one. The state troopers weren't giving them a chance.

The weight of everything hit me so hard my knees nearly buckled.

We weren't going to die here.

I turned to Stiles, and for a moment, we just stared at each other, chests heaving. The adrenaline was still thick in our veins, but the fight was over.

Relief slammed into me so fast I almost laughed.

Stiles let out a long breath, his grip on his empty gun loosening. He looked like he didn't know whether to collapse or start celebrating. "About damn time."

I swallowed hard, nodding. "Yeah."

Neither of us moved for a few seconds, as if making sure this wasn't some kind of cruel trick, some hallucination brought on by exhaustion and fear.

Stiles exhaled, running a hand through his sweat-matted hair. His fingers trembled slightly, the aftershocks of adrenaline still coursing through him.

He let out a shaky breath and jerked his chin toward the tunnel.

"I'm gonna get the others out," he said, his voice raw but steady.

I nodded. "Yeah. Go."

I stepped forward, my boots crunching against the gravel. The night air hit me, thick with the lingering smell of gunpowder and blood. The flashing red and blue lights from the state troopers' vehicles cast jagged shadows across the waterfront.

Bodies lay sprawled across the ground—cartel men, some dead, some groaning in pain, hands gripping gunshot wounds. A few officers were already zip-tying the ones still breathing, their weapons trained on them as they barked orders.

I scanned the scene until my eyes landed on the woman leading the team. She stood near a patrol SUV, speaking into a radio while keeping an eye on the situation. She looked like she was in her early forties, her blonde hair pulled into a tight ponytail, her uniform sharp despite the chaos.

I walked up, clearing my throat. "You're in charge?"

She turned, her gaze sharp and assessing as she looked me over. Her eyes flicked to my empty gun before meeting mine again.

"Captain Emma Freeman," she said briskly. "And you are?"

"Mike Harris." My voice came out hoarse. "I'm with—" I hesitated. "—a team. We were the ones who tried calling this in."

Recognition flickered across her face. "Harris," she repeated. "Right. We got your message, it came through but for some reason, we couldn't get a response back to you." She frowned, shaking her head. "Communications were jammed. We're still figuring out how, but my guess? The Agents from Homeland Security didn't want anyone calling for help." I glanced over to a patrol vehicle and saw two agents handcuffed on the ground next to the car.

"We realized the signal was being interfered with. Either they had a jammer nearby, or someone was blocking outgoing transmissions. But once we got close enough, we were able to break through it and pinpoint your location."

I let that sink in, glancing back toward the tunnel entrance where Stiles was helping the detainees climb out one by one. Raul emerged first, his face tense, his eyes scanning the area as if expecting another ambush. Behind him, Mia guided the others up, her expression unreadable.

I turned back to Captain Freeman. "You got here just in time."

She gave me a look that said she knew exactly how close it had been. "Seems that way."

She motioned for one of her officers, who jogged over. "Get a medic on them," she ordered, nodding toward the detainees. "Make sure they're stable before we start processing statements."

The officer gave a curt nod and hurried off.

Lane crossed her arms. "You armed?"

I lifted my empty gun slightly. "Not anymore."

Her mouth twitched, almost like she wanted to smirk but thought better of it.

"Well, that's a hell of a way to run out of bullets."

I huffed a tired laugh. "Yeah. You could say that."

Behind us, more vehicles pulled up. The second wave of reinforcements. More officers spilled out, fanning across the area to secure the scene.

It was over.

Chapter 9

Raul approached me slowly, his face grim, his eyes shifting between me and Stiles. His hands trembled slightly as he reached into his bag. For a brief second, I tensed—after everything that had happened, I wasn't taking any chances. But when he pulled out a tightly wrapped bundle of papers, a small flash drive tucked into the folds, I exhaled.

"This is everything," he said, his voice hoarse. "Documents. Bank transactions. Names. I recorded conversations when I could. It's all here."

I stared at the bundle, the weight of it heavier than it should've been. This wasn't just a stack of paper or a cheap flash drive. This was proof. Proof of everything we had risked our lives for. Proof that could bring the whole damn cartel down.

Raul swallowed hard. "I held onto it because I didn't know who to trust. But now..." He let out a breath. "Now, I'm trusting you. My life—our lives—are in your hands."

I looked at him, then at Stiles. We both knew what this meant. What this could do. And what could happen if it got into the wrong hands.

Stiles took a step forward, lowering his voice. "You understand this doesn't mean we hand it over to just anyone, right?"

Raul's jaw clenched, but he nodded. "I know. I just—I can't keep running. I need this to end."

I took the bundle, securing it in my jacket. "We'll take care of it."

Raul exhaled shakily, nodding. But as he stepped back, I turned to Stiles.

"We still can't trust everyone," I muttered under my breath.

He nodded, his expression dark. "We've seen the corruption ourselves. We hand this over to the wrong person, and it disappears. Or worse, they make sure we disappear."

The thought settled between us like a stone. We weren't naive. The cartel had people everywhere. Cops, politicians, judges—anyone who could be bought, anyone willing to look the other way. We had survived this far, but that didn't mean we were safe. Not yet.

"We take it straight to the Chief," I said finally. "No one else."

Stiles nodded in agreement, but the tension in his posture didn't ease. We both knew this was only the beginning.

***

The weight of the moment settled heavily in the dimly lit office. The bundle of evidence sat between us like a live grenade, one wrong move away from blowing everything apart. Chief Hughes leaned forward, his elbows on the desk, staring at it as if he were trying to see through the layers of paper, through the ink and recorded voices, into the tangled mess of corruption and violence it represented.

I watched his face carefully. Hughes was a good cop—the kind who still believed in the badge, who hadn't been bought or broken by the system. But even good men had their limits. And this? This was a storm big enough to break anyone.

"This is everything?" Hughes asked, his voice steady but low.

"Everything," I confirmed.

Stiles crossed his arms. "It's enough to bring many", If it gets to the right people."

Hughes let out a slow breath, leaning back in his chair. "And if it gets to the wrong people, it disappears."

"Or we do," I added.

Hughes didn't argue. He knew it was true. He was surprised that we lived what we went through. He was also starting an investigation on why Dispatch didn't do a radio check on us.

He finally reached out, picking up the flash drive, rolling it between his fingers as if testing its weight. It looked so small. Insignificant. But the names on it, the money it tracked, the voices it recorded—they had the power to either change everything or sign our death warrants.

Then Hughes frowned. He plugged the flash drive into his laptop, and the screen illuminated his face in a dull glow. As he scrolled through the files, his expression hardened. His fingers, normally so steady, clenched into a fist on the desk.

And then he cursed.

Stiles and I exchanged a look.

Hughes scrolled down further, muttering under his breath. "Damn it." He shook his head and looked at us. "Do you have any idea how deep this goes?"

"We have an idea," I said.

Hughes let out a humorless chuckle. "No. You don't."

His eyes flicked back to the screen. "This isn't just cartel money. These aren't just random dirty cops or low-level bureaucrats. We're talking high-level law enforcement—people in positions to bury investigations, to control entire departments." His jaw tightened. "Jesus Christ."

He scrolled again, then stopped. His face darkened, and I knew—just from that change in his expression—that he had found something personal.

"What is it?" I asked.

His voice was grim. "I know some of these names."

Stiles exhaled sharply. "Yeah?"

Hughes nodded, his fingers tightening around the mouse. "Detective Jimenez."

That name alone made my stomach turn.

Jimenez was a senior detective in Narcotics. He'd been with the department for years—long enough to have a say in what cases moved forward and which ones got buried. I had worked with him before, and something about him had always felt... off. But nothing concrete. Nothing I could ever prove.

And now?

Now his name was sitting in front of us, alongside payments, dates, and case numbers that had conveniently gone cold under his watch.

"That son of a...," Stiles muttered.

Hughes's eyes stayed on the screen. "And it doesn't stop with Jimenez." He scrolled again, his jaw clenched so tight I could see the muscle twitch. "Agent Morales."

I stiffened.

Morales was FBI. A high-ranking agent who'd worked directly with our department on major cartel cases. If he was compromised, that meant federal investigations—ones that should have taken down entire networks hand in hand with Homeland Security—had been compromised too.

"This explains a lot," Hughes murmured.

I knew what he meant.

We had seen cases fall apart. Witnesses disappearing. Surveillance footage getting 'accidentally' erased. Informants turning up dead. And every time, it had felt like something wasn't adding up.

Now we had our answer.

Hughes closed his eyes for a second, pinching the bridge of his nose. When he opened them again, they were sharp. Focused.

"Alright," he said finally. "No one outside this room knows about this until we verify it."

I felt a small, cold relief settle in my chest. Hughes was taking this seriously.

He tapped his fingers against the desk, thinking. "Who else knows you have this?"

"Just us," I said. "And Raul."

"Good. Let's keep it that way." He leaned forward again, voice firm. "I don't need to remind you, but I will—if we move too fast, we spook them. If we move too slow, they start covering their tracks. And if the wrong people catch wind of this before we're ready, we're done before we even start."

Stiles nodded. "We understand."

Hughes studied us for a long moment, his sharp gaze taking in the exhaustion in our faces, the dried blood and dirt on our clothes, the weight we were carrying after everything that had happened.

Then he exhaled and shook his head. "Damn good work. Both of you."

His voice was firm, steady, but I could hear the undercurrent of something deeper—something like pride.

I should have felt relieved. Maybe even satisfied. But all I felt was tired.

Hughes must have seen it, because he leaned back and said, "Take the next few days off."

I opened my mouth to argue, but Stiles beat me to it. "No chance, Chief."

Hughes raised a brow. "That wasn't a suggestion."

"We're not taking time off," I said, straightening. "Not with this hanging over our heads."

Hughes sighed like he had been expecting that answer.

"Fine," he said. "But at least go home. Get some sleep. Shower, eat something that didn't come out of a vending machine. Because when this starts moving—when the arrests start happening and people start panicking—I'm gonna need you both at full strength. And right now, you look like hell."

Stiles smirked. "Feel like hell, too."

I let out a breath I hadn't realized I was holding. I knew I wouldn't really be able to sleep. Not yet. But I'd take the few hours. I'd let myself breathe—for now.

Because Hughes was right.

This wasn't over by a long shot.

The months that followed were a blur of long nights, endless paperwork, and an unshakable sense of paranoia. Every day felt like walking through a minefield, never knowing which step would be the one that got us blown to pieces.

The case was bigger than any of us had anticipated. Every call we made, every document we pulled, led to another name, another connection— some expected, some shocking. It wasn't just the cartel; it was the people we had worked with, the ones we had trusted, the ones wearing the same badge as us. There were dozens of arrests.

And the deeper we dug, the more dangerous things became.

At first, it was small things—phone lines clicking, files going missing, conversations abruptly ending when we walked into a room. Then it escalated. Witnesses disappeared. Some of the names in the files we had been building—names of officers, agents, politicians—started resigning without warning, moving out of town, vanishing before we could even get to them.

And then there was Raul.

We got the call late one night. Stiles and I had been working in the precinct, piecing together bank transactions, trying to make sense of the mess when Hughes stormed in, his face pale, his jaw tight.

Raul was dead.

Suicide, they said.

But when we got to the scene, it didn't add up.

The room was too clean, the placement of the body too deliberate. The gun, positioned just a little too perfectly. And there were marks—subtle, but there—on his wrists, like someone had held him down before it happened.

It wasn't a suicide.

We all knew it.

But proving it? That was another story.

The case should've unraveled right then and there. The message was clear: If they could get to Raul, they could get to any of us.

Hughes was furious. We all were. But anger didn't stop the system from grinding forward.

And so we kept pushing.

Some of the key players went down. Jimenez got arrested—internal affairs pulled his financials, and everything matched what was on the drive. They found cartel money, fake accounts, a trail that was too sloppy for him to explain away. Morales went missing before they could serve the warrant. Word was, he fled south, deep into cartel territory where no badge would ever reach him.

But not everyone fell.

Some of the biggest names on our list—officials who had been part of this for years—kept their seats, kept their power. They distanced themselves just enough, erased their tracks just well enough, and walked away untouched. They still wore their expensive suits, still shook hands with the public, still acted as if nothing had happened.

And maybe, for them, nothing had.

But for us, everything had changed.

Hughes nearly lost his job. The pressure on him was immense—calls from higher-ups, warnings disguised as friendly advice. The department was bleeding, and someone had to take the fall. They tried to pin it on him, to make it seem like he had lost control, like he had let things slip too far.

But he fought back.

He stood his ground, and in the end, they backed off. Maybe they realized he wasn't worth the trouble, or maybe they just wanted this whole thing buried and done with. Either way, he kept his badge. But we could all see it—the exhaustion in his eyes, the weight of everything he had tried to hold together.

And us?

We did our best.

We worked the case until there was nothing left to work, until the walls that wouldn't break stayed standing, until the missing people stayed missing.

And then, one day, we stepped back and realized—we had done all we could.

It wasn't the ending we wanted.

But it was the one we got.

We did what we could. We did the best we could. But was it enough?

Some nights, I lay awake thinking about Raul. About the way he had hesitated before handing me the evidence, the way his eyes darted around, as if he knew what was coming for him. Maybe he did. Maybe he always knew. And yet, he still made his choice.

In the end, he died for it.

Some days, I could see the weight of it on Stiles. It was in the way he moved, the way he lingered at his desk longer than usual, the way he stared at the scar on his arm without really seeing it.

And then one night, as we sat at a bar—not drinking to celebrate, not drinking to forget, just... drinking—he finally said it.

"I don't know, man," he muttered, his fingers tapping against his glass. "Maybe I'm done."

I glanced at him, waiting.

He shook his head, giving a tired laugh. "I mean, look at all this. Months of work, and yeah, we took some of them down. But how many are still out there? How many are still walking free, still making money off of other people's suffering? We barely scratched the surface. And we lost people for it. We damn near lost ourselves for it."

I stared down at my own drink, thinking.

Because he wasn't wrong.

This job took from you. It broke you down, piece by piece, until you had nothing left. I'd seen it happen before—good cops who started with fire in their hearts, determination in their eyes, only to burn out years later, exhausted and bitter. Some left. Some stayed and let the system mold them into something they swore they'd never become.

And some—some just disappeared, their bodies found in back alleys or burned-out cars, their names whispered as cautionary tales.

I exhaled slowly. "You remember that night?" I asked finally. "When we were in that tunnel? No way forward, no way back. Outnumbered, outgunned. We could've given up then. Just sat there and waited for them to find us."

Stiles scoffed. "Yeah, well, I wasn't about to die in some goddamn hole in the ground."

"Exactly," I said. "We fought. We didn't know if we'd make it out, but we fought anyway. That's what we do."

He didn't say anything, just watched me.

I sighed, leaning back. "I get it, Stiles. I really do. It's tempting to walk away. Hell, I've thought about it too. But if we leave, then what? We let them win? We let them keep running things while we go pretend none of it is our problem anymore?"

Stiles ran a hand over his face.

"I know it feels like we barely made a dent," I continued. "But we did something. We took down some of the people who thought they were untouchable. We sent a message, and maybe we don't get to bring them all down, but if we can take out even one more, if we can stop one more person from getting caught up in their web... isn't that worth it?"

He was quiet for a long moment. Then, finally, he sighed. "Damn it, Mike."

I smirked. "Yeah?"

He shook his head, downing the rest of his drink. "I hate when you do that."

I clinked my glass against his. "Do what?"

He didn't answer. But I saw it in his face—the resolve settling back in, the weight still there but not enough to break him.

He wasn't leaving.

The precinct felt different now. It wasn't that it had changed—same old walls, same desks, same officers walking the halls. But something about it felt...hollow. Like I had finally seen the cracks that had always been there, and now I couldn't unsee them.

I thought about that night, about the tunnel, about the gunfire echoing in my ears. About Raul handing me that drive, his last bit of trust before they got to him. About the cartel, about the corrupt cops who had been working right beside us for years.

Before, I thought I understood what this job was. Serve and Protect. Do the right thing. Bring the bad guys down.

But that night had shown me something else.

Justice wasn't clean. It wasn't a perfect system where the good guys won, and the bad guys lost.

Justice was a war. A messy, bloody war, fought in the shadows, where the lines blurred and the people you trusted could be the same ones who put a bullet in your back.

We had won a battle. But the war?

It wasn't over.

And maybe it never would be.

But as long as we were still standing, we would keep fighting. Because that was the job.

And that was the cost.

The End

In Loving Memory of

ARLEEN M. FREEMAN

07/08/1941 – 10/24/2024

Special Dedication to James W. Freeman Sr. and James W. Freeman Jr. two men who will never be forgotten!!!!

My Small Tribe, Marie, Joshua, Sara, Brian, Darren J., Emma

Veronica, Noah and Bela

9 781734 391183